WONDER BOOKS™

The
Grand Canyon

A Level Three Reader

By Cynthia Klingel and Robert B. Noyed

The
Child's
World®

On the cover...
This picture shows a view of the South Rim
area of the Grand Canyon.

Published by The Child's World®, Inc.
PO Box 326
Chanhassen, MN 55317-0326
800-599-READ
www.childsworld.com

Photo Credits
© Cameron Davidson/Tony Stone Images: 6
© 1997 Darrell Gulin/Dembinsky Photo Assoc. Inc.: 22
© David Muench/Tony Stone Images: 9
© David Young-Wolff/PhotoEdit: 21
© 1995 Dusty Perin/Dembinsky Photo Assoc. Inc.: 14
© 1997 Dusty Perin/Dembinsky Photo Assoc. Inc.: 29
© Gary Yeowell/Tony Stone Images: 13
© Hugh Sitton/Tony Stone Images: 10
© John Beatty/Tony Stone Worldwide: 26
© Larry Ulrich/Tony Stone Images: cover
© Lukasseck/Tony Stone Worldwide: 25
© Mark E. Gibson/Photri, Inc.: 18
© 1993 Terry Donnelly/Dembinsky Photo Assoc. Inc.: 17
© Tom Bean/Tony Stone Images: 5
© XNR Productions, Inc.: 3

Project Coordination: Editorial Directions, Inc.
Photo Research: Alice K. Flanagan

Library of Congress Cataloging-in-Publication Data
Klingel, Cynthia Fitterer.
The Grand Canyon / by Cynthia Klingel and Robert B. Noyed.
p. cm. — (Wonder books)
"A third level reader" —Cover.
Summary: Briefly describes the Grand Canyon, its appearance, history,
how it was formed, and its importance as a travel destination.
ISBN 1-56766-825-9 (lib. bdg. : alk. paper)
1. Grand Canyon (Ariz.)—Juvenile literature.   [1. Grand Canyon (Ariz.)]
I. Noyed, Robert B.   II. Title.   III. Wonder books (Chanhassen, Minn.)

F788 .K59   2000
979.1'32—dc21   99-057846

Do you know where the Grand **Canyon** is? Here is a map to help you find it.

3

The Grand Canyon is a famous natural **landmark** in the United States. It has been a national park since 1919.

These people are riding mules through the Grand Canyon.

The Grand Canyon is in Arizona. Arizona is in the southwest corner of the United States. The canyon covers 1,218,375 acres (493,442 hectares). It is 277 miles (446 kilometers) long. That is huge!

From high above, you can see the Colorado River flowing through the canyon.

The Grand Canyon is made of rock. It was formed by the flow of the Colorado River. The river has worn down the rock along the sides of the river. This has taken millions of years.

This is a picture of Marble Canyon. It is a part of the Grand Canyon.

The Colorado River still flows down the center of the Grand Canyon. The canyon has three parts, called the North Rim, the South Rim, and the Inner Canyon. Each part is very different.

This picture shows a view of the South Rim of the Grand Canyon.

The North Rim is the coldest part of the canyon. It gets a lot of rain and snow. The South Rim is similar, but it does not get as cold. The Inner Canyon is warmer and more like a desert.

Here clouds are floating in part of the North Rim of the Grand Canyon. →

The rock in the Grand Canyon is what makes this a special place. There are many layers of rock. Each layer is a different type of rock. These different layers make a rainbow of colors in the rock.

← The rocks in this part of the canyon look red in the sunshine.

Even though the canyon is made of rock, many plants grow there. Different kinds of plants grow in the different parts of the canyon.

This picture shows some of the plants that live along the South Rim. →

18

Many kinds of large trees grow on the rim of the canyon. Desert plants such as **cactuses** grow at the bottom of the canyon. Beautiful flowers such as **poppies** grow in the cooler parts.

These desert plants grow near the bottom of the canyon.

The canyon is home to many animals. Snakes, **coyotes**, lizards, bats, and skunks live at the bottom of the canyon. **Prairie dogs**, mule deer, squirrels, and foxes live at the top of the canyon.

This deer is eating in a forest at the top of the canyon. →

The Grand Canyon has other animals, too. Deer, porcupine, elk, mountain lions, and bears roam the canyon. Hawks and eagles soar above it.

This bald eagle is looking for food near the Grand Canyon.

People go to the Grand Canyon to hike. It takes two days to hike from the top of the canyon to the bottom and back to the top.

These hikers are walking on a path high above the canyon. →

Some people enjoy rafting down the Colorado River. Other people fish in the river. The Grand Canyon is a popular place for camping. It is a wonderful place to watch wildlife and enjoy the scenery.

This picture shows a group of people steering their raft down the Colorado River.

The Grand Canyon is a very popular place for visitors. Each year, more than 5 million people visit the Grand Canyon. It is one of the most beautiful sights in the United States.

These visitors are enjoying the view from the top of the Grand Canyon.

Glossary

cactuses (KAK-tuh-sez)
Cactuses are plants that have sharp spikes and grow in hot, dry places.

canyon (KAN-yun)
A canyon is a deep, narrow river valley with high sides.

coyotes (ky-OH-teez)
Coyotes are furry animals that look like small dogs.

landmark (LAND-mark)
A landmark is a statue, building, or place that is important in history.

poppies (PAH-peez)
Poppies are plants with large red flowers.

prairie dogs (PRAYR-ee DOGZ)
Prairie dogs are small animals that are related to squirrels and live underground.

Index

To Find Out More

Books

Cone, Patrick. *Grand Canyon.* Minneapolis: Lerner Publishing, 1994.

Minor, Wendell. *Grand Canyon: Exploring a Natural Wonder.* New York: Scholastic, 1998.

Petersen, David. *Grand Canyon.* Chicago: Children's Press, 1992.

Web Sites

Grand Canyon Explorer
http://www.grand-canyon.az.us/grand.htm
For virtual tours of the Grand Canyon area and trail descriptions.

Grand Canyon National Park Service
http://www.thecanyon.com/nps/
For current news about the park and information about visiting the Grand Canyon.

Note to Parents and Educators

Welcome to The Wonders of Reading™! These books provide text at three different levels for beginning readers to practice and strengthen their reading skills. Additionally, the use of nonfiction text provides readers the valuable opportunity to *read to learn*, not just to learn to read.

These leveled readers allow children to choose books at their level of reading confidence and performance. Level One books offer beginning readers simple language, word choice, and sentence structure as well as a word list. Level Two books feature slightly more difficult vocabulary, longer sentences, and longer total text. In the back of each Level Two book are an index and a list of books and Web sites for finding out more information. Level Three books continue to extend word choice and length of text. In the back of each Level Three book are a glossary, an index, and a list of books and Web sites for further research.

State and national standards in reading and language arts emphasize using nonfiction at all levels of reading development. The Wonders of Reading™ fill the historical void in nonfiction material for the primary grade readers with the additional benefit of a leveled text.

About the Authors

Cindy Klingel has worked as a high school English teacher and an elementary teacher. She is currently the curriculum director for a Minnesota school district. Writing children's books is another way for her to continue her passion for sharing the written word with children. Cindy Klingel is a frequent visitor to the children's section of bookstores and enjoys spending time with her many friends, family, and two daughters.

Bob Noyed started his career as a newspaper reporter. Since then, he has worked in communications and public relations for more than fourteen years for a Minnesota school district. He enjoys writing books for children and finds that it brings a different feeling of challenge and accomplishment from other writing projects. He is an avid reader who also enjoys music, theater, traveling, and spending time with his wife, son, and daughter.